# THE SLEEPING BEAUTY

# THE SLEEPING BEAUTY

RETOLD AND ILLUSTRATED BY

## MERCER MAYER

MACMILLAN PUBLISHING COMPANY · NEW YORK
COLLIER MACMILLAN PUBLISHERS · LONDON

*Macmillan Publishing Company*
*866 Third Avenue, New York, N.Y. 10022*
*Collier Macmillan Canada, Inc.*

*Printed in the United States of America*

*10   9   8   7   6   5   4   3   2   1*

*Library of Congress Cataloging in Publication Data*
*Mayer, Mercer, date.*
*The sleeping beauty.*
*Summary: The author/artist has embellished this folk-*
*tale of the princess who sleeps under an evil spell for*
*100 years with some details of his own.*
*[1. Fairy tales.   2. Folklore]   I. Sleeping Beauty.*
*II. Title.*
*PZ8.M4515Sl   1984   [398.2]   84-7195*
*ISBN 0-02-765340-4*

FOR MARY ANN

# THE SLEEPING BEAUTY

Somewhere in time, in a faraway land, there lived a great king in a large castle with many courtiers and servants. Nevertheless, the king was lonely. One day he came upon a stable girl who tended the royal horses. So deeply impressed was he by her gentleness, sincerity, and beauty that he fell in love with her and asked her to become his queen.

Living in that kingdom were twelve faeries with very great powers, so in order to show them respect the king invited them to the wedding feast. Of course, all the noble lords and ladies of the kingdom were invited as well. For days the castle chefs worked at baking and roasting, preparing the banquet. Tables were set up with fine dishes and silver and, at the special table for the faeries, twelve golden goblets, which the king prized most highly.

What the king did not know was that the previous year the manager of his household staff had fallen deeply in debt, and had sold one of the golden goblets, replacing it with gold-painted lead. For, the manager reasoned, the king is so wealthy, and I have served him so many years, how could he mind if he really knew my plight?

On the day of the wedding feast all the lords and ladies and faeries arrived, taking their places at the richly appointed tables. Each guest in turn proposed a toast, the nobles with silver goblets, the faeries with the gold. Finally the time came for the Blue Faerie to make her toast. As she rose from her place, it was clear to everyone that she was very angry. As fate would have it, she was the one served with gold-painted lead. She raised the lead goblet high in the air and said,

"My toast to you and your bride is this:

> *"Never shall you children bear,*
> *For this insult will not repair!"*

The Star Faerie, who had not yet spoken, rose and said, "Good king and queen, I cannot undo a curse but I can modify one.

> *"Never shall you children bear*
> *Until the silver owl appear."*

One by one, the faeries rose and departed.

The king tried to comfort his bride, but to no avail. Finally, at daybreak, he decided he must find the silver owl himself. Bidding the queen farewell, he set off on horseback.

The days turned into weeks as the king searched far and wide for the silver owl. One night before his return, as the queen waited, a silver owl flew into her chamber. In her desire to have a child, she overcame her fear of the strange bird. She fed and cared for it and allowed no one to harm it.

Finally the king returned, and the queen, delighted, showed him the silver owl. Soon after that, the queen conceived a child.

As they waited for the birth, the queen continued to care for the owl, showing it great tenderness. Time passed, and the king began to grow more and more jealous of the attention she paid to the owl. Although he knew the owl must be enchanted, his jealousy finally overcame him and he had the bird killed. He presented the feathers to the queen.

The queen was horrified. "How could you do such a thing?" she cried. "Our happiness began the day the silver owl arrived."

Not wishing to admit to his rage and jealousy, the king replied, "I thought it might escape, and this way you would always have its beautiful feathers."

Soon a baby girl was born to them. The queen took the feathers of the silver owl and made a soft cover for her. The curse of the Blue Faerie remained in her mind, and she hoped the feathers from the enchanted bird would protect the child.

The king remained jealous and angry, but he kept it in his heart. Nevertheless, it consumed him, as though he still lived under the Blue Faerie's curse. When the time came for his daughter's christening, he neglected to invite her, thus offending her a second time.

A procession of lords and ladies arrived for the ceremony, each bearing a gift for the child. Each faerie brought a gift as well; from the Red Faerie came the gift of beauty, from the Orange Faerie, the gift of charm. The Yellow Faerie gave the gift of grace, and the Green Faerie gave the gift of wisdom.

As the ceremony continued, the door suddenly flew open and a great gust of wind swept the hall.

"And I give the gift of death!" cried the Blue Faerie as she appeared in the doorway. "Oh, feeble, mortal king," she said, "not only have you insulted me by not inviting me here today, but you deeply wounded me by killing the silver owl. He was my brother, who had taken pity on you and your wife."

As though a veil had been lifted from his eyes, the king saw his mistake and fell to his knees. "Blue Faerie, have pity now, for the sake of the child!"

"I will show the child the same pity you have shown to me and mine," said the Blue Faerie. "When your child has grown into all the gifts my sisters have given, she shall prick herself with a spindle and die." With that, the Blue Faerie vanished like a cloud of ice-cold vapor.

The queen began to weep softly as the Star Faerie, who had yet to give her gift, stepped forward. "Your daughter shall not die," she said, "but she shall fall asleep until one who loves her more than life itself shall find her and kiss her on the lips. Then she shall awake."

Immediately the king gave orders that all spindles in the kingdom be destroyed. The years passed, and the child grew in all the gifts the faeries had given her. When she reached the age of seventeen, the king arranged a festive birthday celebration for her. After a day of feasting and games, the princess grew weary and slipped away. Soon she came to a part of the castle where she had never been. Curious, she made her way across an empty courtyard to an old tower. She climbed the winding stairs inside and found a small door at the top, slightly ajar. She opened it and entered a little stone room.

There sat the Blue Faerie, spinning. "Oh, let me try," said the princess. Since she had never before seen a spindle, she felt no fear. She took the spindle eagerly, and no sooner had she touched it than it pricked her finger. She fell to the floor in a swoon and lay there as if dead.

When the king realized his daughter was missing, he ordered a search of the castle. Soon they found her in the old tower. Although she was breathing still, nothing would awaken her. They carried her to the great hall and placed her on a small couch. Then the king sent for the Star Faerie.

She arrived on the first morning star. "All of the things that were foretold at her christening have come to pass. If one who loves her more than life itself shall find her, then she will awaken. If not, then she shall sleep until the end of time."

"Then I will order someone to love her," said the king in his grief.

"No," said the Star Faerie. "That is not the way, but you can help."

"Only tell us what we can do," said the queen.

"I will place a deep enchantment here," said the Star Faerie, "and all within the castle gates shall sleep too, so that if she wakes in a different time she will have those she loves with her. Otherwise, if she awakes alone many years from now, when all of you are dead, her heart will break. But understand; if no one finds her, then neither she nor any of you will ever awake again."

Then the Star Faerie cast her spell and left. She had told them that the deep enchantment would come when they least expected it, for that was the only way it would work. A year passed, and still they waited. The princess slept on, and the king and queen grieved deeply for their daughter. When they looked at her, it seemed that she would awake at any moment.

One day at noon, the air around the castle grew still and heavy, as never before. Everyone stopped and wondered at it for one brief moment, and then they fell asleep. The cook fell asleep boxing the scullery boy's ears. The king and queen fell asleep in the throne room. The horses fell asleep in the stable, the dogs in the yard, even a little mouse that crawled out to steal a piece of cheese and was surprised by the cat. They fell asleep together, curled up on the floor. The fire in the hearth slept. Not a breath of wind blew, not a blade of grass stirred. Not a cricket chirped, not a bird sang. Everything was still.

Around the castle grew a great thorn hedge. It grew wide and thick and tall, part of the Star Faerie's enchantment to protect them as they slept. It grew so quickly that within a single hour it covered the entire castle, and within a day it was as high as a mountain. Circling the mountain of thorns there formed a wide, deep swamp, murky and dark and full of quicksand, vipers, and adders. At the edge of the swamp a griffin stood guard, keeping everyone away. Only one who loved the princess from all eternity, without thought for his own life, would ever dare to make his way through this horrible place. And so it had to be, to break the Blue Faerie's curse.

The Star Faerie placed a dwarf on the road leading to the swamp and the mountain of thorns to warn travelers and to test the resolve of any who dared go farther. The castle was rich, and some would come to plunder. There would be those who were simply foolish. But there would be only one who would feel something deep within his soul call to that within Sleeping Beauty.

Ten years passed, then twenty. The Blue Faerie left the kingdom and went to another one, far away. Eighty years came and went. The Blue Faerie enchanted a king. She married him and bore him a son. The boy grew to be a man, and when the one hundred years had passed, he was twenty years old. He had known the story of Sleeping Beauty all his life, and he knew he was destined to search for her.

The prince told his father that he meant to find Sleeping Beauty, but his father forbade him to go. One moonlit night, he slipped away. As he was passing the outer gate, a figure stepped from the shadows. It was his father, who said to him, "As you are a man with his own heart and mind, I know that I cannot hold you. Take this sword, for it is all I can give that might save your life." They embraced and the youth set off.

The prince traveled many miles and through many lands. In each place he asked after Sleeping Beauty, until eventually he arrived in the kingdom where she lay. As he walked through a dark forest, a little man appeared before him.

"Where are you going?" asked the dwarf.

"I am seeking Sleeping Beauty," replied the prince.

"Do you love her more than life itself?" asked the dwarf.

"I am prepared to forfeit my life to find her," said the prince.

"We shall see," said the dwarf. Then out of the shadows stepped one of the most beautiful women the prince had ever seen.

"Please stay with me," said the lady.

The prince knelt before her and said, "Lady, I am at your service, but I cannot stay."

"Then turn and meet my father," she said. The prince turned and found himself face to face with a terrible ogre who came at him with gnashing teeth and sharp claws. The prince drew his sword and cut off the ogre's head, whereupon both the ogre and his daughter vanished into the air.

The dwarf stood laughing behind him. "That was a test," he said. "Many who were filled with desire followed her. Later she ate them. Many were frightened away. Others were filled with greed. They wished to plunder Sleeping Beauty's castle. Their greed was so great that they even came this far. But I always find out.

"If you are true," said the dwarf, "then know that the griffin is no worse than you yourself. The hardest way through the swamp is the easiest. And pity will lead you through the thorns. Good-by." With that, the dwarf was gone.

The prince continued to follow the path through the woods. Soon he came to a barren land, rocky and dry. In the distance he saw the griffin standing guard. I'll wait until dark to try to pass him by, thought the prince. But each time the prince tried to go by him, the griffin woke with a mighty roar. Then I will try to approach from the north, thought the prince.

After seven days of travel, he was north of the forest, but the griffin was there as well. He tried to approach from the east and the west, but each time the griffin was waiting.

There is no way to get around the griffin as he sleeps, thought the prince. I will approach while he is awake and battle to the death, if necessary. As he neared the beast, the griffin roared and beat his wings. The prince drew his sword and came closer. To his surprise, with every step he took the griffin grew smaller and smaller. By the time they were face to face, the griffin was the size of a large dog. Indeed, thought the prince, the dwarf was right. The griffin is not as he appears.

Before him lay the swamp. The prince entered it, walking on whatever dry land he could find. Along the way he saw vipers and other strange creatures that called him by name. He saw monsters in the mist and reflections in the murky water. He stumbled over swords and pieces of armor from earlier travelers who were now lost forever to the swamp. In the floating mists, dreamlike visions beckoned to him. A weak heart would have turned to stone, but the prince fixed his mind and heart on Sleeping Beauty to keep from going mad.

Gradually the prince began to realize that if he turned toward the beautiful visions, the way grew harder and more treacherous. But if he turned toward the monsters and walked through the pools of horrible creatures, his footing was surer. The way grew easier, until finally he reached the edge of the swamp.

The thorns were sharp and thick. The prince carefully picked a way around the edge, trying to find a way through them. He passed skeletons in the thorns—the remains of those who had become entangled in them and died. His heavy boots crushed a small thorn bush and the vines began to tighten around him, but with each torturous step the way before him opened more and more. At last he stood before the castle gate.

Within the walls of the castle the thorn bushes flowered into beautiful roses. The prince wandered through the rooms of the large castle in wonder, seeing everyone there asleep. He could wake no one. Finally he reached the flower-covered chapel. He pushed the door open and entered. A golden ray of sunlight fell upon a small couch at the foot of the altar. There, on the couch, lay Sleeping Beauty. She could be no other, for his heart burned within him. He approached, knelt down, and kissed her on the lips.

Sleeping Beauty stirred, opened her eyes, and said to the prince, "Who are you? I must have fallen asleep. Have the others gone home?" She thought it was still the day of her birthday celebration, when she had gone to sleep. The prince could not speak, he was so glad to have found her.

Soon the whole castle awoke. The king and queen rushed to the chapel to see their daughter. With cries of joy they embraced her and then the prince, as though he were a son.

The prince was taken away to bathe and have his wounds bound up, while the queen explained to Sleeping Beauty what had happened. "He loves you more than life itself," said the queen, "and that is why he came."

"Mother," said Sleeping Beauty, "I also love him more than life itself. As I slept, I dreamed he was trying to find me. In some dreams he was a boy and in others a man. But in my dreams I always knew he would come."

Not long after that day, another splendid feast was held in the castle, this time for the wedding of the prince and Sleeping Beauty. Invitations were sent to the nobles of the kingdom, and to the faeries as well. But no invitation was sent to the Blue Faerie, for she could not be found.

On the appointed day, all the guests arrived, but it was a very different celebration from those the castle had seen so many years earlier. The lord and ladies huddled together in groups and whispered, for they were in a castle that had been shut off from the world for one hundred years. Nor had they ever before seen faeries, for during those hundred years faeries had withdrawn completely from mortal company.

While the feasting continued, the Blue Faerie arrived at the castle. Knowing what was in her son's heart, she had followed him, planning to prevent the wedding. As she approached the gates, she heard the sounds of celebration. The realization that she was too late filled her with more anger than any mortal can know. Throwing open the doors, she stormed into the great hall.

"Again you have offended me!" she cried. "Not only did you not invite me, but you have tricked my son into marrying your daughter."

The prince was astonished to see her standing there, for he did not know his mother was the Blue Faerie. The king and queen shuddered, for it seemed they would never be free of the Blue Faerie's curse. Her voice rose in rage.

*"My blessing here can never be,*
*For I shall take my son with me.*
*Ashes to ashes and dust to dust,*
*All mortals die and so they must.*
*A curse I place upon this spot:*
*All those with mortal blood shall rot."*

"Mother," said the prince, "if you curse this household, then you curse me also, for I am now bound to this family by marriage. And if you curse me, your own blood, then you curse the blood of all faeries. And one faerie may never curse another. Your power here is broken by this marriage. I shall never go with you!"

The faeries in the room stood and faced the Blue Faerie. The Star Faerie, the last to come, was last to speak.

"You have broken a faerie law.

*"If one faerie is by another faerie cursed,*
*Then all the evil is reversed.*
*It will haunt you down and be your own,*
*For you must reap what you have sown."*

The Blue Faerie grew white with fear. In her anger, she had gone too far.

Sleeping Beauty spoke to the faeries. "There is another law that is stronger. It is the law of forgiveness. All has ended well, and I forgive my husband's mother."

"I will not be forgiven by a mortal!" the Blue Faerie screamed. She stormed out of the hall, followed by all the evil she had ever wished on others. Where she went, no one knows. Some say that the evil eventually destroyed her. Others say that after many years she returned to her mortal husband and begged forgiveness from her son and his wife. It is also said that to this day she has lived in a convent, praying to be made mortal and thereby set free by death.

The prince and Sleeping Beauty had children. Being of both mortal and faerie blood, they grew fairer and more quickly than most. Their children and their children's children ruled wisely and gently for another century or more.

The Star Faerie and her kind seldom returned, preferring to keep their distance from mortals.

In the later years, the prince who became king chose to be mortal in order to stay with his queen, Sleeping Beauty. In the vaults of time they are buried together, but beyond time they live in eternity as we all shall do.

J

N M

398.2 Mayer, Mercer
M

The Sleeping Beauty

| DATE | | | |
|---|---|---|---|
| | | | |
| | | | |
| | | | |
| | | | |
| | | | |
| | | | |
| | | | |
| | | | |
| | | | |
| | | | |
| | | | |
| | | | |
| | | | |
| | | | |
| | | | |

© THE BAKER & TAYLOR CO.